I Was There...

TUTANKHAMUN'S

TOMB

While this book is based on real characters and actual historical events,
some situations and people are fictional, created by the author.

For Sarah Selous, with thanks for her friendship

Scholastic Children's Books
Euston House,
24 Eversholt Street
London, NW1 1DB, UK

A division of Scholastic Ltd
London ~ New York ~ Toronto ~ Sydney ~ Auckland
Mexico City ~ New Delhi ~ Hong Kong

First published in the UK by Scholastic Ltd, 2015

Text copyright © Sue Reid, 2015

Illustrations by Michael Garton
© Scholastic Ltd, 2015

ISBN 978 1407 14888 5
Printed and bound by CPI Group (UK) Ltd, Croydon, CR0 4YY

1 3 5 7 9 10 8 6 4 2

I Was There...
TUTANKHAMUN'S
TOMB

Sue Reid

CHAPTER ONE

It was me who saw them first. We'd gone up the mountain to search for treasure. I'd just crawled, bottom first, out of a cave. I hadn't found anything. Either the magician was wrong, or Ahmed had got the wrong cave. Ahmed was doubled up laughing.

"You do look funny!" he said. I stood up, shaking myself like a dog. "It's not funny!" I said. It was always me who got the dirty jobs! All the same I'd been glad when Ahmed had turned up to ask Uncle if I could help him find their lost goat. Anything was better than a day in the field guiding the buffalo round the water wheel. Uncle agreed to let me go at once – goats are precious. It was only when we were halfway up the mountain that Ahmed told me the real reason he'd come to fetch me – we were going to look for treasure!

A famous magician had come to the village a few days ago to help one of the villagers find the treasure he thought was hidden somewhere on the mountain. He hadn't found it, but Ahmed said he'd told him secretly where it was. I wasn't sure I believed him. Ahmed often makes things up. Like that lost goat.

He poked his head into another cave. "Let's try this one," he said. "It's got to be here somewhere."

There were hundreds of caves on the mountain! It could be in any one of them. I shook my head. "I'm going back," I said. I began to climb over rocks and boulders, dropping down to a goat track. Grumbling,

Ahmed jumped down after me. The track was narrow and in places took us very close to the edge. Stones crumbled under my feet and bounced away down the mountain. I kept my eyes on the path. If I slipped, I had a long way to fall.

I walked cautiously over to the edge to see where we were.

I nearly toppled off the cliff! I was looking almost straight down on to the tomb of Pharaoh Ramesses VI!

In front of it men were digging, heaving up big stones and carting them away.

The Valley of the Kings, where the ancient Egyptians had buried their pharaohs, was the other side of the mountain from our village. We'd climbed a lot further than we thought.

I grabbed Ahmed's arm. "Look!" I said excitedly.

He shook me off. "What is it?"

"Come and see!"

I'd gone back over to the edge to take another look.

"What? There?" He looked at me uneasily.

I was very near the edge.

"Hurry up!" I was getting impatient.

Ahmed shuffled up to me. A snail would have crawled faster. He peered down cautiously.

"Can't you see?" I said. "It's the Valley of the Kings down there. They've come back to find the tomb."

"So?" said Ahmed. He wasn't as interested

in our past as I was. Me, I could name all the pharaohs whose tombs had been found in the Valley.

"There'll be treasure!" I said, sprinting off down the path.

"Gold necklaces!" Ahmed shouted, bounding after me. You just had to say treasure and Ahmed would be off like an arrow.

Who knew what we might find. Even if it was only bits of old pot, we could sell them. Lots of people came to look at the tombs in the Valley, and they always wanted souvenirs to take home. They'd buy anything they thought was old.

Last year I'd sold them a pot Mother had thrown out in the rubbish. It wasn't old. My brother had made it, and I had broken it. We'd made a lot of money from it that day.

There was just one problem. How were

we going to get down there? We didn't dare try the main route – guards patrolled that to keep tomb robbers out. Of course, we could carry on along the goat track. But there were loads of tracks, criss-crossing the mountain. We might not be on the right one.

There was one other way. We could climb down. I went back over to the edge again. We weren't far to the ground here, and there were plenty of boulders and rocks for us to hold on to. "I'm going to climb down," I called to Ahmed.

Without waiting for him, I launched myself over the side of the mountain, testing each rock and stone with my hands and feet before putting my weight on it.

I'm a good climber. Grandfather calls me "little goat". I'd earned the nickname the day he'd caught me climbing down into an underground tunnel. Mother had been furious when she'd found out. "Never do that again," she'd scolded me. "You could fall or wake the *afarit*! How many times have I told you about the bad spirits that live underground?"

So I didn't tell her about the time I'd climbed down the shaft at the back of our tomb home. Our home, like the homes of many of the people who live in the hamlets on the foothills of the mountain, is built out of an ancient tomb. Grandfather says I'm lucky to live there.

"You sleep in one of the tombs where ancient Egyptian nobles were buried," he'd told me. It was where I'd found the *shabti*. A shabti is like a tiny mummy. Father used to make them before the knife slipped and cut off one of his fingers. The ancient Egyptians put shabtis in the pharaohs' tombs to serve them in the Afterlife. Father had sold his to tourists who came to see the tombs.

I'd tucked the shabti into a fold of my robe, then climbed up again to show Grandfather. Grandfather had told me it was thousands of years old.

"Look," he'd said, pointing at the hoe it was holding. "See that? This shabti would work for his master in the fields."

"Like me?" I'd said.

Grandfather had smiled. "Like you, but he would have done what he was told!"

I glanced back. Ahmed had left the path and wasn't far behind me now. Ahmed was a good climber, too. He'd soon catch up with me.

I was about three quarters of the way down when the stone I was clinging to slipped out of my grasp and bounced away down the mountainside. I felt my stomach plummet inside me. In a minute that could be me! Ahmed was just behind me now. I grabbed wildly for his foot as I shot downwards. Next minute we were both rolling down the mountain together. Ahmed slid down on top of me and we bounced down the last few feet.

"That was a stupid idea!" Ahmed grumbled, picking himself up carefully. I got up, too. I felt as if I'd been shaken all over, but it hadn't been a bad fall. We hadn't been that far from the bottom when I slipped.

"At least the guards didn't see us!"

"That's because only an idiot would do what you did!"

I didn't answer. Shielding my eyes from the glare of the sun, I gazed over the Valley, searching for where the men were digging. I soon saw. It wasn't far.

"Come on!" I said.

We tore across the Valley, our bare toes leaping over the hot sand. Even in November the Valley is hot and airless. In summer it's like being shoved head first into an oven.

It didn't take us long to reach the dig. We walked around the pit they'd dug out, peering down into it to see how far down it went. It was impossible to tell. A dusty cloud swirled upwards, and hid the bottom. Boys ran up and down, removing the rubble in baskets, vanishing and appearing again like phantoms.

I asked one of them what they were doing. Dark eyes peered at me from a face smeared with dust and dirt. "Mr Carter thinks there might be a tomb under one of those ancient huts. See those?" He jerked his thumb at the boulders the men were carting away. "That's them. What's left of them. They were used by the workers who built Ramesses VI's tomb." Grandfather had told me there were still three royal tombs that hadn't been found – those of pharaohs Smenkhkare, Ramesses VIII, and Tutankhamun. It was Tutankhamun's tomb I wanted them to find. Grandfather had told me that Tutankhamun had been about my age when he became pharaoh. I often wondered what that must be like. To sit on a throne and get everyone to do what you wanted!

"Why does he think he'll find it under a hut?" I said.

"Because he's looked everywhere else!" The boy laughed and disappeared back into the pit.

Howard Carter, a British archaeologist, had come to dig in the Valley year after year. Few people believed he'd find a tomb now.

Next to me Ahmed yawned. "I'm bored," he said. "We won't find anything here. The foremen will see us. Let's look through the dump."

We'd seen the dump as we'd run up to the dig. All the rubbish that was being dug up was piled on to it.

I shook my head. "You go," I said. "I'll catch up with you later." Now I was here I wanted to watch. Besides, I didn't think we'd find any treasure there. Before the rubbish was tipped on to the dump it was sieved and inspected carefully. Even small bits of pot were taken out and put on one side to be examined.

Ahmed shrugged. "Thought we'd come to look for treasure," he said.

Leaving Ahmed to poke around the rubbish, I settled down to watch, keeping a wary eye out for the foremen. I'd already spotted two. One was watching as the rubbish was sieved. Another was yelling at the basket boys to get a move on. I'd chosen a spot behind a heap of stones near the dig where I could see what they were doing without them seeing me. But every so often a cloud of dust billowed out of the pit towards me and I had to run back, too.

Voices rose and fell from the pit. They sounded cross.

"Where's the water carrier?"

"Mouth's as dry as a tomb."

"I'm thirsty."

The voices were getting louder. I realized it was because they were getting closer. I ducked down just as one of the diggers reached the top. He looked cross and hot.

"When will we get our water!" The digger threw down his shovel, and wiped his face with his sleeve.

"Be patient!" The foreman looked harassed. "The lad's not here yet."

"Well, where is he then?"

More diggers climbed out of the pit and came to join the group by the foreman. The mutterings increased.

And then I had an idea. I could sneak off and hope he wouldn't spot me. On the other hand...

I wanted to stay, didn't I? Maybe this was my chance. I stepped up to the foreman's side.

"Let me fetch the water, Effendi," I said, careful to add that title of respect. He might be more likely to hire me then.

The foreman wheeled round and stared at me. "Who are you?"

"Ali, Effendi." I bowed low.

"How will you fetch the water?"

I hadn't got a donkey, but I had my answer ready.

"I can carry it on my head," I said. I hitched up my robe, trying to look bigger and stronger.

The foreman folded his arms. I saw his lip

curl. I waited for him to send me packing. I'd been stupid to think he'd hire me.

"Wait!" I heard an amused voice say. Someone was watching us. He was almost as dusty as everyone else but he was no workman. It was Howard Carter, the man leading the search for the tomb.

Sometimes I'd seen him ride his donkey up the mountain on the way to his house. I'd never been there, but men who had talked about a big house with a dome that was cool in summer and warm in winter.

I bowed my head respectfully as he reached us. He gave me a thoughtful look, idly picking at a tooth with his finger.

"He can use my donkey today," Mr Carter said. "The men need water, and there's no sign of the other lad. Tomorrow he can bring his own."

The foreman had opened his mouth to

say something but at Mr Carter's words he shut it again. Mr Carter was the boss.

I bowed again, as Carter strode back to the dig. We had a donkey. I was sure Father would let me have it when he knew I had a job.

A donkey was brought up to me, a water jar strapped to each flank. "Mind you behave yourself," the foreman warned as I climbed up onto its back. I dug my heels into its sides. I'd got a job! What was Ahmed going to say when I told him? And maybe I'd be here when they found that tomb!

CHAPTER TWO

The sun was sinking behind the mountain when I got home. I slunk into the courtyard. I knew I'd be in trouble. All the way home I'd been trying to think what I'd say. Mother was the first person I saw. She was crouching in front of the oven, feeding maize stalks into the furnace below. She jumped as if she'd seen a ghost.

"Ali," she cried, "where have you been? We were worried about you." Her eyelids looked red as if she'd been crying. "And look at the state of you!" she exclaimed. "What have you been doing?"

"Rolling down hills by the look of him!" Father growled behind me. He seized me by the collar of my robe and swung me round to face him. He gave me a shake. "The truth, now!"

Uncle had already been to Ahmed's house to look for me, he said. "Your little friend told him you had a job fetching water for Mr Carter." He snorted. "A likely tale."

Ahmed had left the Valley hours ago. Empty-handed. Unlike me.

"It's true, Father," I said. I held out my hand. In it were the coins the foreman had given me – earnings for my day's work. Father would have to believe me now. Maybe he'd even be proud of me.

"What is that?" Father said, releasing me and peering at the coins.

"It's my pay," I said. And there'd be more tomorrow, too!

"Hmm," said Father. "You expect me to believe that? How did you carry the water?"

"On Mr Carter's donkey. But tomorrow I'll take ours."

"You will, will you? How will we manage without it?"

I felt my face grow hot. Father had to let me go. They were expecting me. "But I gave them my word!" I protested. Besides, I'd earn money – money we needed now that Father could not make beautiful things any more. The pots my brother Hassan made were no better than anyone else's. Neither of us had inherited Father's talent.

"Don't speak to your father like that," Mother said, turning round from the oven. A delicious smell wafted from it. My mouth watered. It was a long time since I'd eaten. One of the men had shared his food with me – half a loaf of bread and a mouthful of wilted onion. "You brought us water, and so I give you food," he'd said. While we ate he'd told me about the golden bird Mr Carter had brought with him from Cairo to keep him company at night. "It will bring us luck," he had said. "This year we will find a tomb full of gold."

"Surely we can manage without the donkey for a few days." I turned to see Grandfather hobble out of his sleeping chamber. Grandfather spent most of the day asleep now, but the smell of a good meal always woke him up! He winked at me. "Maybe he will bring us luck. And he has brought us money today. And there will be more tomorrow, eh, Ali?"

Father looked at him. Then at Mother. She was nodding. Mother was the true boss of the house.

"Very well," he said at last. "You may go and take the donkey."

I gave him a grin. "Thank you, Father!"

"But only for a few days. I will need it back to take the pots to market."

A few days! Mr Carter had been searching the Valley for years. It could be many days before he knew if he was digging in the right place.

"If they haven't found the tomb by then, they never will," Father said firmly, as if he knew what I was thinking. I knew Father thought that Mr Carter was wasting his time. That he would never find Tutankhamun's tomb. Mr Carter wasn't the first man to have come searching for it. Even us, the mountain folk who knew more about the Valley and its secrets than anyone else, didn't know where it was. That secret was buried with the boy-king.

Grandfather sniffed. "That smells good. Are you as hungry as I am?" I took his arm to help him sit down, then helped myself to bread that Mother had piled high with beans for me. When we'd finished, Grandfather turned to me and smiled. "So, little goat, you want to find the tomb of the boy-king." He put his head near mine, and said in a whisper that only I could hear. "And you will. Do not believe what others say."

"But when, Grandfather? I will only have the donkey for a few days!"

"You will find him," he said. He kissed the top of my head and I curled up close to him. I loved Grandfather dearly. I couldn't think how he knew, but I felt sure he did.

"Will you tell me about Tutankhamun, Grandfather?" I asked.

Grandfather chuckled. "What more can I tell you? He was only a lad like you when he became pharaoh. That was thousands of years ago...." He sighed. "Soon he will be taken from us. As they all are."

Grandfather always talked about Tutankhamun as if he were still alive. He tried to explain about the sacred *ka.*

"Is it like my *karin*?" I said.

"A little," he said.

Grandfather had told me that all Egyptians were born with something he called the karin. "You can't see it," he'd said. "It's invisible to human eyes. Think of it as your double – exactly like you in every way."

I looked up at Grandfather's face as he continued. "But unlike the karin, which dies when you do, the ka lives on after death. By day it leaves the tomb, but at night it must return there. If anything should happen to harm the mummy, then the ka has no home to go to, and the soul will die."

I felt myself shiver.

"Soon there will be nothing living left in the Valley – save vultures, bats and snakes."

There were tears in Grandfather's eyes. I put my hand on his.

He began to tell me about the day the mummies of several pharaohs were taken away to the Egyptian Museum in Cairo. It was a story he'd told me many times before but I liked hearing it as much as he liked telling it.

"We ran down to the river to watch. Oh how the women wailed to see them go! I cried, too. The men fired their rifles, saluting the pharaohs as the barge bearing their mummies passed by. My father picked me up and sat me on his shoulders so that I could see. I was a child like you then. It was on that day that I first became fascinated by our wonderful past."

I felt my head droop on Grandfather's shoulder. Grandfather put his arm round me and gave me a squeeze. "It is time for bed, little goat. You need to wake early. You have a great day ahead of you!"

I crawled into the chamber I shared with my brother and curled up on my sleeping mat. On one side, a mud brick wall separated us from the pen where our donkey and other animals were kept. The other wall was solid rock. Behind me the tomb stretched deep into the hillside. I reached out my hand and took out my shabti from its hiding place, behind a loose stone. "I am your master now," I said to it. "Don't you forget. In the morning you will guide me to the Pharaoh's tomb."

"What on earth are you saying?" In the moonlight I saw my brother Hassan duck down to enter the chamber. He grinned.

"Nothing. Let me sleep!" I hid my shabti under the blanket till I was sure Hassan was asleep, then slipped it back into its hiding place. Grandfather was the only person who knew about it. If Hassan found it, he'd make me sell it.

I didn't hear Father or Grandfather slip past us into their chamber. I heard and saw nothing more till morning when the light woke me. Excitement twisted inside me. I was going back to the Valley!

CHAPTER THREE

"Get up, you lazy creature!" I hissed. I tugged the donkey's mane again. It looked at me grumpily. It wasn't going anywhere in a hurry!

By the time I'd got the beast up, everyone else was waking up, too. Hassan stumbled half asleep out of our chamber. Mother gave me some food and helped me strap the water jars on to the donkey's back. I was in a tearing hurry now. If I was late, the foreman would give my job to someone else.

I climbed up on the donkey's back and headed up the mountain. Noise and chatter came from the tomb houses around me. The village was waking up. Two women walked past me on their way to the well, water jars on their heads. One of the village dogs uncurled itself from a heap of rubbish to sniff at us. Behind me I heard a cockerel crow. I wondered if Ahmed would come down to the Valley today. He was lucky – he didn't have to work as hard as me. He had four older brothers to help with it.

I turned on to the path that led to the Valley. At least I didn't have to scramble over the mountain today. The guards jumped up when they saw me and pointed their guns at me. They asked me what I was doing there.

I held my head high. I am Effendi Carter's water carrier, I told them. They laughed, waving me on with their guns.

Before I reached the Valley, I was joined by diggers and basket boys. They told me they were pleased to see me. "We will have plenty of water again today."

"We will need it!" one of the men said. "It is hot work, digging up all that rubble!" He told me that Mr Carter thought there might be a stairway hidden underneath it. A stairway that led to the tomb!

I left them while I went to fill the jars at the well. While I drew up the water, I thought about what they'd told me. There was a lot of rubbish to clear away; it could be ages before they found the stairway. I just had to hope they'd find it soon. I only had the donkey for a few days. After that, I'd have to go back to working in the fields and helping Hassan sell his pots.

I poured out water for the men, then sat down nearby to watch, wrapping a corner of my turban over my nose and mouth. Dust from the dig got into everything. No one took any notice of me. I was Ali the water carrier now, and they didn't seem to mind me. Besides, their eyes were fixed on the ground as they shifted great piles of debris into baskets. Everyone wanted to be the one who found the hidden staircase!

I was sifting sand idly through my fingers when my hand hit something hard. I scrabbled down a bit deeper. Maybe I'd found a bit of old pot, though it felt more like a stone. Probably one the diggers had missed when they were carting them away. I bent down to pick it up, but it was stuck fast. I dug deeper, until I could feel its edges. I began to feel excited. Maybe I'd found what everyone was looking for!

My heart began to beat hard.

I jumped up. "Hey!" I cried, waving my arms. "Come here. Quick!"

The men nearest me swung round to me. "Hey, Ali, what are you doing over there – get off with you now."

They wouldn't mind, not when they saw what I'd found!

"I've found a step! Look!" I bent down and jabbed a finger at the stone.

"What's he saying?" One of the men put down his pickaxe and came over to me.

I pointed at the stone I'd uncovered. "It's a step. I've found the hidden staircase!"

I crouched down and ran my hand over the stone. "At first I thought it was just an ordinary stone, or a bit of rock, but see…"

The man's eyes followed my finger as I drew it round its edges.

"Don't get too excited. It's just a stone, lad."

"No," I said. "You're wrong. It's the entrance to the tomb. I'm sure it is."

I was practically shouting now. The commotion brought other men to my side.

"He's right!" a voice exclaimed next to me. I stepped back as the foreman crouched down and ran his fingers over the stone, too. A rare smile broke on his face. He stood up again and waved us away. All work was to stop, he ordered, until Mr Carter arrived.

It was almost ten o'clock before I saw Carter ride up to us. By then I was about to burst with excitement. "Is something wrong?" he said, climbing down off his donkey. "Why have the men stopped work?" The foreman scuttled up to him. I scowled at his back. I felt sure he was telling Mr Carter it was him not me who'd found the step.

He took him over to where I'd found it. Carter looked doubtful as he bent down. But he'd been digging in the Valley for years. Often he must have thought he'd discovered something only to find he was wrong.

He ran his hand over the stone. No one moved. No one spoke. Everyone's eyes were fixed on him, waiting to see what he thought. I held my breath. Was it a step? Or wasn't it?

He sat back on his heels, and I saw him look up at the sky, a big smile on his face, the kind of smile you make when you've been given the most wonderful present.

Then he stepped back, pulled out a notebook, and wrote something in it. "Back to work now," the foreman said to the men. They picked up their tools to start digging again – right where I'd found that stone!

I heard a shout. Two boys ran up to me. "We've been at the dump," Ahmed said breathlessly, flinging himself down next to me.

"Hallo, Ali," the other boy said slyly, sitting down on my other side. It was Ahmed's brother Salim. I wished Ahmed hadn't brought him. I didn't trust Salim. He had shifty eyes and hands that were never still.

"Someone told us they've found a step. Is it true?"

I nodded. "I found it," I said proudly.

Ahmed whistled. "Perhaps it will lead down to the tomb."

"And treasure." Salim's eyes gleamed. So that was why he was here. To find treasure. I might have guessed. It was the only thing he cared about.

"Where is it?" Ahmed asked. "Show us, Ali."

"It's where they're working," I said.

Only now I saw they weren't. They'd stopped again and were leaning on their tools.

I jumped up. "They might have found another step," I said excitedly. "Let's go and see."

"It's probably just a bit of rock," Salim yawned. "Come on. Let's go back to the dump."

"No wait," said Ahmed. "Ali's right — it might be important."

We squeezed up to the men to see what they were looking at.

I could see a steep cut in the bedrock, about four metres below the entrance to Ramesses' tomb.

"Just a bit of rock. Told you so," Salim said. "Come on, Ahmed!"

"Let us know when you find the tomb, Ali!" Ahmed said as they ran off. I went back to my seat. I knew it was important, even if they didn't. Mr Carter was pacing up and down, arms behind his back. I could see that he was as excited as me. After years of finding nothing it was wonderful to think we might be on the brink of an amazing discovery.

The men began to dig again, even faster than before. Everyone was excited.

Load after load of rubble was carted away to the dump. The foreman's whip cracked at the heels of the basket boys. "Faster! Faster!"

When they stopped to eat, one of the men explained what they'd found.

"That cut in the rock," he said. "It means it really might be the top of that stairway we've been looking for."

My heart beat faster. And at the bottom of it might be Tutankhamun's tomb!

"Of course we can't be sure," he said. "Not till all this lot has been cleared away."

I was kept busy that afternoon fetching water. The men were working very hard and were hot and thirsty. Each time I got back I asked them if they'd found another step. I always got the same answer. "No. Just rubbish, lad. There's a lot of it to clear away. But we'll find another step soon. Now how about some of that water!"

At the end of the day they were still clearing the rubbish away. I wished they'd hurry up. In a day or two Father would want his donkey back. "It's a good sign," one of them said, wiping sweat off his forehead. "All this rubble will have kept robbers out!"

I climbed on to my donkey's back. Salim and Ahmed were still investigating the dump. I didn't wait for them to come back.

I wanted to be the first to get back to the village. I wanted to be the first to tell everyone about the step. It was me who'd found it, after all!

CHAPTER FOUR

The street was busy as I trotted down it. It was the time of day when people left their homes to chat and share news. Just wait till they heard mine! That would give them something to talk about. I looked out for the men of my family. I was bursting to tell everyone what I'd found. But I wanted Grandfather to hear it first.

I jumped down off the donkey's back and led it through the courtyard to the pen. Then I ran back into the courtyard.

Father and Grandfather were leaning back against the wall, eyes closed, under the awning of palm leaves Hassan and I had made in the spring. Mother was sweeping the courtyard. Hassan was bent over the pot he was moulding, cursing the lump of clay in his hands.

Just wait till they knew! How astonished they were going to be. Father would be so proud of me. And Grandfather… Grandfather would say he'd always known.

"I found the step," I said into his ear. "The step that leads to the tomb," I added, just so he knew what I was talking about, even though none of us knew that for sure yet.

Next to him Father opened one eye. "What did you say?" he said. He gave Grandfather a gentle push. "Wake up," he said. "Ali has something to tell us." Grandfather opened his eyes and smiled at me, as if he already knew.

Father shifted up so I could sit between them, and I poured out all that had happened that day.

They listened quietly throughout, nodding their heads every so often. When I'd finished Grandfather whispered: "I knew you'd bring them luck! And one day you will see inside the tomb itself!"

I asked him how he could be so sure.

"Because it is written, little goat," he said.

Grandfather often talked like this – as if he could see into the future. Maybe he was right. Maybe I would see inside the tomb!

He got up and hobbled out of the courtyard into the street. "Come!" he said. "I must share the news with my friends."

"And I will tell mine," said Father. He laid a hand on my head. "I am proud of you, Ali," he said. I felt happy. It wasn't often Father told me that he was proud of me. Mother smiled at me and put down her broom. "It is a good day for the village," she said.

Hassan merely grunted, before throwing

down the lump of reddish clay and picking up another. Hassan was never pleased about anything I did.

I ran outside. Grandfather was sitting on a bench next to some of the old men of the village. He beckoned to me. "Here he is. Now we will let Ali tell us what he found, just as he told it to me."

In my village, you can't keep a secret for long! Soon I was surrounded by a jostling crowd, all eagerly asking me questions.

"They might have found the entrance to the tomb. Aiee! After all these years, too!"

I found it hard to get to sleep that night. Tomorrow we'd find out. If only the night would hurry up and end. If only the moon would go down and the sun come up!

"Lie still and let me sleep, Ali!" Hassan grumbled, turning away from me. "Some of us have to work you know."

"I work, too!" I protested.

Hassan snorted. "You call that work! Fetching water and sitting around waiting for a tomb to be discovered. Make sure you get your share of the treasure when it is!" He laughed, but I didn't think it was funny. I huddled as far away from him as I could.

Soon I heard a gentle snore. Hassan was asleep. I lay there, gazing out at the stars. Somewhere, on the other side of the mountain, lay the boy-king. But how long would it be before we found him?

CHAPTER FIVE

"Goal!" shouted Ahmed. I looked down to see the ball dribble between my feet. Salim had found an ancient waterskin in the rubbish yesterday and had sewn it into a ball. We'd used big stones to mark where the goalposts were. One or two of the basket boys who weren't needed had come over to play too.

"You weren't even looking!" Ahmed complained, running over to fetch the ball from me.

I kicked it over to him, and went to sit down near the dig. I wiped my forehead with a corner of my turban. We'd been kicking the ball around for ages. It was too hot to play now.

The sun beat down fiercely. My donkey huddled miserably by my side.

I'd just found a dung beetle and was searching for another to race it when I heard the men talking excitedly. I leapt to my feet and ran up to see what they'd found. One of the diggers made room for me. "It's a sunken staircase all right," he said. "The kind that leads to important tombs. You can see all the upper edges of it clearly now. Soon we'll find out where it goes. Ha!" He lifted his pick and swung it at the rock.

I asked him how he could be so sure. "Why, lad, I've been digging in the Valley for years. I know an ancient stairway when I see it!"

And it would lead us to Tutankhamun's tomb. I knew it, we all did, though no one said it aloud.

Step after step was being dug up now. Excited messages were whispered up them from boy to boy.

"How many have they found now?"

"Four."

"No, you're wrong, it's five."

Soon they'd dug up a lot more than that.

About halfway down, the staircase became a passage, roofed in by the rocky hillock where Ramesses had his tomb.

"It's high enough for me to walk under, and as wide as this," one of the men said, as I poured out water. He stretched out his arms on each side to show me.

But how long would it be before they reached the bottom? The sun was beginning to sink behind the mountain, spilling gold across the Valley. It wouldn't be long before it set. Even the top steps were bathed in shadow now. Mr Carter had come up once or twice to gaze anxiously at the sky. Soon it would be too dark for the men to work. It felt like a race against time.

Ahmed and Salim appeared out of the shadows to sit beside me. "Have they got to the bottom yet?"

I shook my head.

"How many have they dug up now?"

I shrugged. I'd given up trying to count them. "Let's go and see," Ahmed said. We got up to look once more. It was very dark down there now. We couldn't see the bottom.

"Ugh!" said Salim peering down. "I wouldn't want to go down there."

"Might be met by King Tutankhamun himself!" said Ahmed as we climbed back up the pit.

"Or his mummy," said Salim. He fell backwards on to the sand and crossed his arms on his chest.

"What are you doing?" I said.

"He's Tutankhamun's mummy," said Ahmed.

Salim rolled his eyes and opened his mouth. "I am the voice of the dead king," he said. "You must obey me!"

Ahmed giggled, but I felt uncomfortable. "Don't talk like that," I said. "You'll bring us bad luck."

"He's dead, Ali. It doesn't matter!" said Salim, sitting up and shaking sand off himself.

I was silent, but I didn't like it. There was something about this place, something that

I couldn't quite explain, but I felt almost as if Tutankhamun could hear us!

On the steps the boys had begun to fidget. The baskets by their feet were empty. "They must have reached the bottom," I said. Ahmed went to the top of the steps to peer down them again. Suddenly he jumped back.

"What was that?" he said, nervously.

"Stop fooling around," I said. I'd had enough of their stupid jokes.

"I really did hear something," he protested.

"It's only someone digging," said a boy on one of the lower steps.

"Didn't sound like that to me," said Ahmed.

The boys looked uneasily at each other. "Spirits," one said nervously. "They've woken the *afarit*."

"I told you, it's just them digging," the boy on the step said again. Only now he didn't look so sure.

"But they've stopped working," another pointed out. We looked at each other. He'd only said what we were all thinking. I just wished he hadn't.

"They've found the tomb," said Salim, going to look down, too. "I can see a light down there. It's him – he's coming for us…" He ran back to us, rolling his eyes and clutching Ahmed in mock terror.

"Don't be an idiot!" Ahmed said nervously, shaking him off.

"Go and see if you don't believe me."

"No fear! You can!"

"All right!" Salim marched back to the dig. On the steps the boys were frozen, like statues. I saw Salim's face change.

"It's him," he shouted, eyes wide with terror. "I can see him." He leapt back, nearly knocking me over.

As one, we turned and fled, tumbling over each other in our haste to escape. It was their fault, I thought. They shouldn't make jokes about the dead.

We were still running when I heard a voice bawl: "Oi! Where do you think you're off to?" We skidded to a halt and turned round sheepishly. One of the diggers was standing at the top of the steps. "Scared you, did I?" He grinned. "Thought I was Tutankhamun, did you?"

His eye fell on me. "You, you're the water

carrier, aren't you? Any water left in those jars?"

I nodded.

"Then fill up this flask and get down here quick!"

What had he said? I swallowed. The man thrust an empty thermos flask into my hands. They were trembling as I tipped water into it. I was eager to know what they'd found, only I didn't want to go down those steps. Not now. It was like being asked to walk into an open mouth.

"Say hallo to Tutankhamun for me," Salim grinned.

Why did he have to say that?

The man shone a torch down the steps so I could see, but I reached out a hand for the wall. The steps were steep and I didn't want to slip. Stones skidded under my bare feet. My heart was swinging inside me like a hammer. I knew it was silly to be scared. I was used to tombs, after all I slept in one, but this was different. We were the first people to walk down these steps for thousands of years. And it wasn't just that, it was what lay beyond them. I cursed Salim – it was his fault for putting ideas in my head.

On the twelfth step I stopped. Mr Carter was crouching on it, his back to me. In front of him was what looked like a door. Only the upper part of it was visible. A heap of rubble hid the rest. Carter wasn't bothering about that now, and I wouldn't if I were him either. I'd want to know what was behind it.

"Have you got the water, lad?" he said.

I nodded.

"Give it to me."

I handed him the flask. He swallowed a mouthful, then put it down and wiped his mouth with his sleeve. "That's better," he said. I saw a small hammer and a chisel on the step next to him.

He flashed his torch up at the door. My eyes followed the beam as it travelled slowly across it. I could see curious things stamped on the plaster. One of them, the oddest of all, was a man with the head of a jackal. Under his foot cowered nine people, bound like prisoners. I drew in a deep breath. What did it mean? Mr Carter swung round to me and smiled.

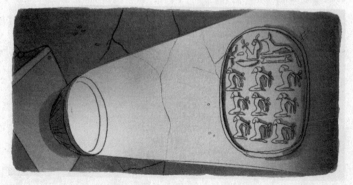

"That, my boy, is the seal of the Royal Necropolis. It tells me that this might be the tomb of a very important person."

It seemed that Mr Carter didn't dare say the name Tutankhamun. He'd been disappointed too often.

"Of course, it may mean nothing…" he said to himself. "There should be other seals." I heard him sigh.

To me it seemed very small for the entrance to a royal tomb. Of course, the door would probably be a lot bigger once all the rubble had been cleared away. They'd find more steps too, leading deeper and deeper…

Carter handed me the torch. "Do you see that small hole in the corner, under the wooden lintel?"

I nodded.

"I'd like you to shine the torch on it. And hold it steady."

He picked up the chisel and began to chip away at the hole. The plaster was loose and came away easily. I began to feel excited.

Soon the hole would be big enough to look through.

Maybe he'd let me look through it, too. I might be one of the first people to see what was inside the tomb!

"Give me that torch. Quick!"

Carter grabbed the torch from me and inserted it through the hole. "Aha!"

What could he see? My mind began to reel. Gold. Heaps of it. Maybe even the coffin of Tutankhamun himself!

Carter withdrew the torch. "Good!" he said. "Very good!" It was then I saw what was on the other side. Nothing. Nothing but rocks and blocks of stone, from floor to ceiling. My mind spun in disbelief. Had Carter seen something I hadn't? How could finding a tunnel blocked up with rubble be good news? He gave me the torch to hold again, and I watched as he filled in the hole.

He caught a glimpse of my face. "Don't look so downcast, lad, there's a tomb there, all right, behind that rock. We'll find it one day. Of course," he added, "we don't know yet whose tomb it is. The evidence should be here somewhere…"

He put on his spectacles and flashed the torch slowly over the door again. Something was missing. Something that would tell him for sure that this was Tutankhamun's tomb. He sighed and stood up. "Come on, lad. It's late." He bounded up the steps, and I stumbled up behind him. I still couldn't understand why that heap of rubble behind the door made him so sure he'd found the tomb.

As I got to the top I saw Mr Carter go over and speak to the foreman. The foreman nodded and beckoned to the men. Broad grins spread over their faces. They picked up their tools. A minute later stones were rattling back over the steps!

I watched in disbelief. Why were they shovelling back all the rubble they'd spent days clearing out?

Ahmed and Salim appeared at my elbow. Ahmed looked as stunned as me. "What are they doing that for?"

I shrugged. How could I know?

"So there's nothing there?" said Ahmed.

"No," said Salim. "You're wrong. It'll be something good. They wouldn't bother filling it all in again otherwise." I stared at him. Salim didn't know it, but he'd just given me the answer to what had been puzzling me. Of course! The tunnel underground had been filled in to protect the tomb from robbers. Somewhere behind that door lay the king surrounded by his treasure. Carter knew what he was doing. Me, I'd been so sure we'd find it behind that first door, I hadn't stopped to think.

Not only were we about to uncover a tomb, but an unplundered one, too! I turned away to hide the big grin that spread over my face.

"Come on," said Ahmed. "It's not a secret, is it?" He sounded hurt.

"Just rubbish," I said and shrugged.

"Is that all?" Salim said. He looked like he didn't believe me for one minute.

"It's all I could see," I said. "Mr Carter

made a hole in the door where the plaster was loose…" I stopped. I didn't like the greedy look in Salim's eyes, like a vulture who'd spotted a juicy carcass. "It's rock," I said. "Lots of it. That's all."

I cast an uneasy glance upwards. The sun had gone down and the moon taken its place. None of us mountain folk liked being in the Valley after dark. "Let's go," I said.

I climbed on to the donkey, pulling on its mane to turn it round. I was about to set off when the foreman called me to him. I trotted over, wondering what he wanted.

He dropped a few coins into my hand. My pay! I'd nearly gone home without it. Father would not have been pleased if I'd arrived home empty-handed. I bowed my head. "Thank you, Effendi."

He hadn't finished.

"We won't need you tomorrow," he said.

I reeled on the donkey's back. What had he said?

"But – the men –"

The workers would have to dig up all the rubble. They'd be hot and thirsty. Who'd bring them water, if not me?

"But –" I said again. I'd been helpful, hadn't I? Why didn't he want me back?

"Work on the tomb is stopping till Lord Carnarvon arrives from England." He puffed out his chest.

From England! All I knew about England was that it was at the other end of the world from Egypt. Lord Carnarvon must be a very important person if they had to wait for him. It'd be weeks before he got here. Weeks before anyone discovered what was on the other side of that sealed door. And judging from the smirk on the foreman's face, he didn't want me there when they did.

I turned my donkey away from him, and headed it towards the mountain. I barely needed to touch my heels to it to coax it forward. The donkey didn't like it there any more than I did. Long shadows crept out of the tombs towards us. At night the Valley belongs to the dead.

Salim and Ahmed had gone on ahead, but I soon caught up with them.

The glow from the guards' fire winked at us from the mountain, but we didn't need it to help us find the right path. The donkey knew its way home now. Ahmed and Salim whispered to each other, but I didn't care. I had other things on my mind.

Now I'd seen the door and knew what might lie behind it, I had to find a way to come back. I wasn't going to miss what I was so close to seeing. No one – not even the foreman – was going to keep me away.

CHAPTER SIX

I gave the buffalo a thwack with a palm leaf.
A cloud of flies flew up before settling back
down again on the buffalo's sweating back.
It turned its head to me and grunted. Like
me, it had had enough of walking round
and round the waterwheel.

At the end of the field, the river swam lazily past. Boys shouted and splashed among the papyrus reeds near the bank. I slumped down by the wheel and fanned my hot face with the leaf. I wished I could have jumped in and joined them. I wished I were anywhere but in that field, working for my Uncle. Uncle was a kind man but he was childless and he kept me busy.

It was over two weeks since work on the tomb had ceased. It felt like a year.

Each night I made a mark with the end of a burnt twig on the wall in my chamber. It was one day nearer to the day Lord Carnarvon would arrive from England, I told myself. But it didn't make the days go any faster.

Ahmed had been down to the Valley once. He'd found a better way down, he'd said, one that didn't involve rolling down the mountain. He'd told me the men had uncovered more ancient huts. I'd made him promise to tell me when Lord Carnarvon arrived. I never had a chance to sneak away. There were always lots of jobs for me to do. When I wasn't helping Uncle in the field, there was water to fetch, buffalo dung and maize sticks to collect for fuel, or the pots to mind that Hassan laid out to dry in the sun.

"Ali! Ali! Quick!"

Ahmed and Salim were jumping up and down at the edge of the field. I dropped the buffalo's rein and ran to meet them, leaping over the newly ploughed furrows. Their being here could mean only one thing. Lord Carnarvon had arrived in the Valley.

"They're here!" Ahmed said as I reached them. "They've begun to clear the passage."

I clutched his arm. "Are you sure?"

Ahmed shrugged. "That's what they said."

"Who said?"

"The boys. I saw some of them coming back from the Valley yesterday."

"You'd better hurry if you want that job back," Salim said.

I cast a glance at Uncle. He'd reached the end of a furrow and was turning the oxen round.

"We're going down there now," Salim added.

"Come later!" Ahmed urged. "They'll be there till sunset."

It was probably too late now. If they'd already begun work, they'd have hired another boy to fetch water for them.

I left the boys and ran back across the field. Uncle was driving the ploughshare back towards me. "What did those rascals want?" he

71

growled. Ahmed wasn't his favourite person since the story about the missing goat.

I could ask, couldn't I? He could only say no.

"Mr Carter is back working in the Valley," I said. I looked up at him hopefully.

"And you want me to let you go, too, don't you?"

I nodded.

Uncle grunted. "I'm sorry, Ali. I need your help here today." He hesitated. He'd seen my face. "Ask your father tonight if you may go tomorrow," he said. "Maybe I can spare you for a few days. Now — return to that buffalo, before it tramples my field!"

"What? Will I let you go back to the Valley tomorrow?" Father said that evening, raising his eyebrows. "No, I need the donkey. Besides, there may not be a job for you.

And there is plenty of work for you here."

"Could I not take the donkey for one day? Maybe they will give me work again, like before," I pleaded. "I will earn money!" Had Father forgotten that I was paid to carry water? And I gave him every coin I earned.

"See this?" Father said. He picked up a pot. "And this." With his other hand he reached for a handful of maize. "These make more than they pay you for fetching water."

"I might find something to sell. An ancient pot perhaps. A … a golden earring. Even a pair!" Somehow I had to persuade Father to let me return to the Valley.

Father shook his head. "And what did you find last time?" he said. "Nothing. No. I need the donkey. And I need you. In a day or so, well, let us see." I pretended not to care, but by bedtime I'd made a plan. Early in the morning before anyone was up I was going down to the Valley. No one was going to stop me. I'd found the step and I was going to be there when they opened the tomb, too.

CHAPTER SEVEN

The sky was beginning to lighten when I woke. Next to me, Hassan stirred in his sleep and muttered. I sat up slowly, careful not to disturb him, and crept quietly out of the chamber. The peak of the mountain looked as if it had been painted pink. Everyone would be up soon – I'd have to hurry! I crept past the pen where the animals were tethered. The donkey turned its head and looked at me. If only I could take it with me.

I ran up the path that wound through the village. Soon I was climbing up the mountain. By jumping from boulder to boulder I managed to dodge the guards.

The sun was almost up when I reached the Valley. I sat down near the entrance to wait. When the workers arrived I'd slip in among them.

It wasn't long before I saw them. They gave me a cheerful wave. "Hallo, Ali, where have you been?"

They'd missed me, they said. The new water carrier was lazy. They never had enough to drink.

At the dig, I left them to slip behind a heap of loose chippings. I didn't want the foreman to see me and order me away. The steps were still wrapped in shadow – 16 had been dug up now. I looked around. It wasn't the only thing that had changed. They'd been busy.

All the workmen's huts had been cleared away. Heaps of chippings fringed the path like foothills. Ahmed and Salim were there, burrowing through one of them.

They waved me over. "We found good stuff here yesterday," Ahmed said. "Things one of the men must have stolen," put in Salim. He grinned. "They're not as good at hiding things as me!"

"Come and help us," Ahmed said.

I crouched down next to them, keeping one eye on the dig. The men had gone down the steps and opened a wooden grille at the bottom, which had been erected where the sealed door had stood. I wondered how long it would take them to finish clearing the passage behind it – and what they'd find when they had.

"It's them!" Ahmed said.

I turned to look. A small party was riding towards us, Mr Carter at their head.

Salim pointed out a skinny man, riding just behind Carter.

"That's him. Lord Carvan."

"Lord who?"

"I think that's his name," Salim said vaguely. "It's something like that."

He meant Lord Carnarvon, I thought. The man who'd come all the way from England. The man we'd had to wait for.

"And that's his daughter," said Ahmed, pointing out a young woman riding by his side. There was another man in the party. "That's Mr Carter's assistant, Mr Callender," said Ahmed.

They'd found out a lot. Servants trailed behind the party on foot. One of them was leading a dog. "That's Lord Carvan's dog," Salim grinned. It was tall and lean like its master – quite unlike the scrawny creatures that hung around the village. "They should send him into the tomb to sniff out Tutankhamun."

Ahmed giggled. "He might have more luck!"

I wished they wouldn't joke about it. It wasn't funny.

The party reached the dig and began to climb down off their donkeys. Carter ran over to help the girl. Lord Carnarvon was climbing down as if he found it difficult. Leaning on a cane, he made his way over to the tent pitched near the dig. A boy pulled out chairs for him and his daughter. Carter and Callender disappeared down the steps.

They didn't look as cheerful as I'd expected.

All morning, basket after basket of rubbish was passed up the steps. When were they going to reach the end of the passage? How far did it go anyway? It could run for miles, twisting and turning all over the Valley, leading… where?

I watched as the sun rose higher and higher. If only they'd hurry. Over in the tent Lord Carnarvon was slumped in his chair, eyes closed, as if he'd given up hope.

The basket boys came up to eat their lunch. Ahmed and Salim had gone back to the dump. I sat down next to the boys, and they told me what they'd found in their baskets. Fragments of painted vases, the handle of an alabaster jar. Fragile, delicate things. The men were having to dig slowly so as not to damage anything. They'd even found a whole vase. Best of all, when they'd dug down to the sixteenth step, they'd found the seals of Tutankhamun on the door.

"But they're still not sure if it is his tomb," one of the boys said. I felt my mind reel. Why not?

"There was a green carved beetle – a scarab – in my basket yesterday," he explained. "Mr Carter said it was an amulet that belonged to Pharaoh Tuthmosis III."

"They've found things that belonged to other pharaohs, too," another boy said.

I felt my heart sink. What if it wasn't a tomb at all? What if it was just a place where ancient Egyptians hid their treasure? I'd disobeyed Father – and it might all be for nothing.

It had been plundered too, they said. That was why they were finding so much stuff among the rubble. Some of the rubble didn't match the rest either. Robbers had broken in at least once. And later the door had been replastered and resealed.

I tried not to think about it, the robbers blundering around in the passage, grabbing what they could, dropping stuff as they fled down the dark and silent tunnel.

A few weeks' ago Carter had seemed so sure he was on the brink of finding a royal tomb. Now it seemed he might be back where he started.

The boys returned to work and I went to find Ahmed and Salim. They nodded when I told them what I'd heard. "They won't have got it all out," Salim said. "Look at all the stuff they dropped!"

As if that was all it was about.

I bent down and dug through the rubbish with my fingers. What was I going to say when I got home? Father was going to be very angry with me. But maybe he'd forgive me if I could find something to sell – an alabaster vase or even the handle of one.

I was on my way back from the dump, empty-handed still, when I saw Carter sprint up the steps, a broad grin under his bushy moustache. My heart gave a big thump. Something was up! Seeing him, Carnarvon sprang out of his chair. The little group went into a huddle. Were we about to get the answer to the riddle that had puzzled us all for weeks? I wished I could hear what they were saying!

"Have they found it?" Ahmed and Salim had seen Carter too, and run over to join me.

"I don't know," I said. I kicked at the

sand with my foot. The excitement I'd felt had begun to fizzle away. Who cared what they'd found. Whatever it was, I'd never get to see it. Grandfather wasn't right this time.

"They're going down!" Ahmed exclaimed. I looked up to see the party walk down the steps, followed by the foremen.

And I had to watch and wait like everyone else.

"We'll learn what it is soon," Ahmed said. I didn't want to learn what they'd found – I wanted to see it!

A breeze sprang up. The tent flapped lazily. The empty chairs underneath seemed to mock me. On the table next to them lay some papers and… a flask. In their haste one of them had forgotten their water. I stared at it. I had an idea. More than anything I wanted to see what lay at the end of the passage. And here was my chance.

An underground passage that hadn't been entered for thousands of years would be hot and airless. Whoever had left that flask behind would be pleased if I took it to them.

I jumped up, ran across to the tent, and snatched up the flask. I shook it. It was half full.

I'd go down there now. Before I lost my nerve. Before it was too late.

Gripping the flask I half ran, half slid down the slope to the steps.

Work had stopped and the men and boys were standing around in groups, talking excitedly – those that weren't staring down the slope towards the steps. Waiting for news. At every moment I expected someone to bellow at me to go back. But no one did. It was as if I'd become invisible.

I stood at the top of the stairs, gazing down them. I swallowed. I had no light to help me this time. Halfway down I could no longer see my feet. Sixteen steps down I banged into the wooden grille. No wonder no one had called me back. That wooden grille had been built to keep intruders out. Like me. I fumbled for the catch. It was probably locked, but I had to find out. To my amazement the door swung open. They'd been in too much of a hurry to remember to lock it.

You will see inside the tomb, Grandfather had told me. I'd begun to think he'd been wrong. But maybe he'd been right, after all.

CHAPTER EIGHT

I groped for the wall, feeling rough stone under my fingers, and shuffled slowly forwards. It was even darker and hotter in the passage than I'd expected. It seemed to be getting deeper, too. Sweat streamed down my back. Now I knew what it felt like to be buried alive. Sharp stones bit into my feet. Voices bounced back along the passage towards me, and the beam of a torch flashed up ahead. I must be getting near the end. Relieved, I hurried towards it. Too fast.

My foot skidded on a loose stone. I flung out a hand, grappling wildly at the air as my feet slid from under me. I twisted my body over to the side so I wouldn't hit my head as I fell. Pain shot up me as I thumped to the ground.

I'd just managed to get up on to my knees when a light flashed full on me. I cowered like a rat, caught in its beam.

"Who's there?" a voice said.

They'd taken me for a tomb robber. I was for it now.

"Get up!" the voice said.

I got up slowly, feeling bruised all down one side. A row of startled faces stared at me. Beyond them I caught a glimpse of a door, almost exactly like the one that had been at the bottom of the steps.

"Why, it's our water carrier!" exclaimed Mr Carter. He lowered the torch a little. "What are you doing here, lad?" His voice was stern. I quaked, I had no right to be there. Over by the wall I saw the foremen, fury blazing in their eyes.

Then I remembered the flask. There was only one thing to do. I bowed and held it out so they could see it. "I… er… I brought water for the Effendi. One of the gracious Effendi left his flask behind. I thought he might be thirsty."

I saw Carter turn to the others.

A burst of laughter echoed down the passage. "Bring it here, lad," Carter said. I began to walk slowly towards him. But before I could reach him, a bony hand shot out and grabbed the flask from me.

"Give me that!" the foreman hissed. "Now – I don't know how you got in, but you can go out the same way."

"Wait!" Carter said. "We need candles. Send the lad for them."

Before anyone could say anything to change his mind, I was hurtling back down the passage.

If only Ahmed and Salim could see me now!

It didn't take me long to reach the steps. I slipped through the grille and hollered up to the men at the top. "Candles – we need candles. Hurry!"

A copper face peered down at me. "Wait," it said. A few minutes later, a handful of sticky wax candles in my hand, I was racing back along the passage. Dodging neatly round the foremen, I slipped up to Carter's side. Carter picked up a hammer and began to chip a hole in the door. I watched as the flakes of plaster drifted down into a basket. Soon we'd see what lay behind that door!

Carter put down the hammer and picked up an iron rod. The hole he'd made was just big enough for the rod to fit through. I watched as he slid it in, testing what lay behind, if anything. I kept my eyes fixed on it until I saw Carter's fist flat against the door. The rod had gone all the way in, right to its tip.

My heart gave a big thump. Whatever was behind that door, it wasn't rubble.

"Pass me a candle, boy! Quick! Quick!" Carter clicked his fingers impatiently. "Before we go any further, I need to make sure that there are no poisonous gases in the chamber."

I fumbled for one that hadn't already melted in the heat. Carter grabbed it out of my hand, lit it with trembling fingers and held it up to the hole. A flame sputtered fiercely in the blast of hot air that gushed out. It smelled heavy, and sweet with ancient spices. Carter had a smile on his face as he handed the candle back to me. "It didn't go out!" I heard him say. "The air in the chamber is pure. It is safe to carry on. Ha!"

He began to chip away at the door again. Flakes and lumps of plaster crumbled down. I noticed that the patch of plaster he was attacking was a different colour to the rest. Robbers had broken through this door, too, making a hole that someone had patched up later. It couldn't have been a big hole, but a small boy like me could have crawled through it easily.

I tried to imagine the scene. The boy slipping through the hole into the chamber, hastily grabbing whatever he could, passing the precious things back through the hole to his gang. They'd be small things: jewellery, coins, boxes, vases like the alabaster vase that had been found in the passage, things that were easy to carry, then sell or melt down. My heart sank. When Carter was finally able to see into the chamber, would there be anything left to see? The hole was too small for robbers to carry out anything large but they may have forced another way in that we hadn't found yet.

Was there even one tomb left in the Valley that hadn't been broken into?

But I still didn't know if it was a tomb. And if it was, whose was it? Carnarvon had switched on the torch and now I could see the door clearly. I bent closer. Strange symbols were written on it. I'd seen symbols like that before, on my shabti. It was ancient Egyptian writing. But what did the symbols mean? I looked back at my companions' faces. They looked excited. They knew all right.

"Tutankhamun," I whispered to myself. Behind that door I felt sure was the tomb Carter had so long been searching for.

"Quick! Give me that candle!" Carter seized it from me and pushed it through the hole. The flame danced and flickered. He moved it lower. The chamber must be some feet lower than the passage, I guessed. All I could see was the back of his head.

What could he see? Why didn't he say?

Was the chamber empty, plundered thousands of years ago?

I heard someone clear their throat.

"Can you see anything?" Carnarvon's voice trembled.

Carter let out a deep sigh.

That sigh might mean anything. Anything at all.

We waited. I thought I'd burst. *Please!*, I begged him silently. *Tell us!*

"Yes," he said at last. "I can. Wonderful things!"

CHAPTER NINE

Carter withdrew the candle and turned round. He looked dazed, as if he didn't know where he was. He handed the candle to Carnarvon so he could look through the hole, too. What he saw seemed to have the same effect on him. He leant back against the wall, as if he needed it to hold him up. One by one they all looked through. Everyone – except me. They were silent, as if a spell had been cast over them.

Carter began to chip away at the hole again, until it was big enough for him and Carnarvon to look through at the same time. I heard a click as the electric torch was switched on. I still couldn't see anything.

But what did they care? To them I was just the boy who fetched and carried their water. It wasn't fair. Would I have to go back without seeing anything at all? "What did you see?", Ahmed and Salim would ask me. And I'd say "Nothing. Nothing at all." I slumped down by the wall, wishing I'd left that flask where I'd seen it, on the table. I wanted to see the wonderful things they had. It was my right. Tutankhamun was my king!

I glanced up. Carter and Carnarvon had turned away from the door, and gone into a huddle with the others, the foremen fussing around them. They'd forgotten me.

Now was my chance. I crept up to the door and thrust my candle through the hole, gazing in eagerly.

At first I couldn't see anything at all. The hot air in the chamber made the candle flicker. Shadows danced on the wall. Strange shapes began to appear out of the gloom. I gaped as I swung the candle from side to side. I could hardly believe what I was seeing. The chamber was crammed with precious things, and gold – gold everywhere. I felt dizzy. Just wait till I told Ahmed and Salim!

There were golden couches shaped like monstrous beasts that looked so real I half expected them to turn and snap their jaws at me. An upturned chair wobbled on top. Boxes below. A heap of overturned chariots and wheels that must have been taken apart to fit them in. Vases. A golden throne. A black shrine out of which slid the head of a huge golden snake. My mind spun in wonder.

I swung the candle further to the right. Someone was standing there silently – a tall, dark-skinned boy, gold kilted and sandalled. One hand held a mace, the other a staff. Big staring eyes gazed into mine. On his golden headdress reared a cobra.

By the sacred cobra you shall know a king of Egypt, the words Grandfather had once told me echoed in my skull.

"Tutankhamun!" I gasped. In my hand the candle hissed like a snake and went out, plunging us into darkness. I dropped it with a cry and stumbled backwards.

I heard someone curse, then a hand grabbed me, dragging me back by the neck of my robe.

"What do you think you're doing?" the foreman hissed.

"Tutankhamun!" I said. "Tutankhamun! I saw him!"

"Bah! That was just his statue you saw."

I felt my cheeks burn. To think I'd been frightened of a statue!

The foreman gave me a shove. "Go! I don't want to see you here again." He didn't need to tell me a second time. I tore down the passage and erupted into the sunshine, a huge grin on my face, my fears left behind in the passage. I'd been into Tutankhamun's tomb! Just wait till they knew!

The boys were hanging over the pit. They

flung themselves on me.

"You were a long time in there!"

"Is it the tomb? Is it? Is it?"

I reached for a water bottle and drank thirstily. My mouth felt as dry as the desert.

"Tell us!"

"It's the tomb all right," I said. "I saw inside it, too!"

They gazed at me in awe.

"What did you see?"

"Wonderful things!" I said.

"Did you see the mummy?"

"Does it smell?"

"Ugh!"

I wiped drops of water off my chin.

"Come on – tell us what you saw!" Ahmed pulled at my arm.

"Gold!" I said. "Heaps of it!"

I tried to describe it. "Huge golden couches, with the heads of wild beasts." I screwed up my eyes trying to remember. They weren't like any animal I'd ever seen before. "As big as…" I studied the pit below us. "About half the size of the pit."

"Go on with you!"

"Don't believe me if you don't want to," I said, reaching for the bottle and taking another gulp.

"What else? What else?" the boys clamoured.

"Chariots, golden boxes, vases, a throne, and…" I was about to tell them about the statue, but I stopped. I don't know why. It was just a statue. I'd been an idiot to be frightened. But I didn't like thinking about it. I didn't like the way those eyes had stared at me.

"And?" Salim demanded.

All right, he'd asked for it.

"And a snake, a giant snake!" I got up

and ran towards him, hissing like a snake. He jumped back.

"You're joking!"

"Was it alive?" Ahmed asked.

"What do you think?"

"Weren't you afraid in there?" Salim asked, his sly eyes flickering over me.

"Afraid? Of course not."

They gazed at me, respect in their eyes. I felt as if I'd grown several feet taller. I, Ali, had been inside Tutankhamun's tomb!

"Come on," I said. "Let's go." Work had stopped for us that day, not that I had any to do. And I wanted to tell my family what I'd seen. They were never going to believe me.

We raced across the Valley, whooping and somersaulting.

But as I got nearer to my home, my feet began to falter. The boys had run off and now I had to face my family.

What were they going to say when they saw me?

I had run off to the Valley without their permission. Would they forgive me when I told them where I'd been and what I'd seen, or would they punish me?

I'd soon find out.

I crept into the courtyard. Father pounced on me and shook me like a rat. "You scamp!" he said. "What have you got to say for yourself?" He didn't ask where I'd been. He knew all right.

"I blame those boys," he said, letting me go at last. "They're a bad influence."

"Oh, Ali," Mother said sadly. I hung my head. I wanted to crawl away and hide.

Grandfather was sitting on the bench. "Don't be too hard on the lad," he said. He leaned forward, his eyes searching mine. "He's looked on things that none of the rest of us have."

Suddenly I felt as if I was back in the tomb, staring into that dark sombre face. I shivered.

Grandfather hobbled over to me and took my hands in his. "Don't be afraid," he said.

"I saw his face, Grandfather," I whispered. "At least... I thought it was. They said it was a statue. But... it was so real."

Father looked from Grandfather to me.

"You speak in riddles. What are you saying?"

"He's seen inside the tomb," Grandfather said, releasing my hands.

"You've been inside the tomb?" Father shook his head as if he was trying to clear it.

"Yes, Father."

"Tutankhamun's tomb?"

"Yes, Father."

He gave a sigh. "I should punish you

but…" He shook his head again, as if he was still trying to make sense of what I'd said. "A son of mine has seen inside the tomb of Tutankhamun. My son. My Ali."

One or two men were passing outside. At Father's words they stopped and stared at him. Then at me.

Suddenly I found myself at the centre of a clamouring crowd. "It is true, then? They've found the tomb? You have seen inside it? What did you see? Has it not been plundered?" I felt myself lifted up on to a man's shoulders and carried down the street. Everyone had heard the news now and ran up to gaze at me, touch my robe and ask me questions. Again and again I had to tell them what I'd seen. I held my head high. I felt like a hero. Like a king!

Then Father called me in and we sat down to eat.

I hadn't thought I was hungry until then. It was our usual fare – bread and beans. Tonight it felt like a feast. In the street a boy began to sing. A drum beat out the melancholy melody, then the reedy notes of a pipe took up the tune. I could still hear it later as I curled up on my mat and tried to sleep. I lay there smiling to myself. I had been inside Tutankhamun's tomb!

CHAPTER TEN

"It was you," a voice whispered. "You. You who led them to my tomb. You who showed them where it was." Strange staring eyes gazed into mine. I'd seen those eyes before. In the tomb. It was him. Tutankhamun. But this was no statue. This was the King himself.

I shrank back in terror. Why was he here? What did he want with me?

"You brought them to my tomb," he said again. He raised his staff and pointed it at me. "You showed them where it was."

I got on to my knees and bowed my head to the floor. "I am sorry, highness," I whispered. "What can I do?"

He was silent.

I raised my head slowly from the floor. The big eyes of the pharaoh still gazed into mine, his face growing larger and larger until it filled the chamber. In terror, I reached out one hand to the wall for my shabti. Maybe it would protect me from this fearsome thing. My fingers closed on bare rock. The shabti wasn't in its hiding place. Someone had taken it away. Then I saw it. It was standing next to me. It bowed to the pharaoh.

"Master!" it said. "Master!"

It would not help me.

I tried to scream but my mouth was dry.

I jerked awake, sweat pouring off me.

I opened my eyes. Moonlight filled the chamber and I could see everything clearly. Next to me, Hassan was curled on his side, asleep. I craned cautiously over my other shoulder. There was no one there. I felt behind the stone for my shabti. It was there, just where it should be. I clutched it gratefully.

It had just been a dream. A bad dream.

I lay down and tried to go back to sleep. But as soon as I shut my eyes, the pharaoh's face swam before me again, his huge eyes gazing sorrowfully into mine. I tossed from side to side. How could I sleep? I'd told everyone about the tomb. I'd boasted about what I'd seen! Even now people might be plotting to rob it. At night it would be easy for a party of men to surprise the guards and overpower them.

It wasn't only robbers that Tutankhamun

needed protecting from, but men like Carter and Carnarvon too, men who would empty the tomb of its treasures and take them and Tutankhamun away.

There was only one thing for it. I had to try and put right what I'd done, and there was only one way to do it. I had to go down to the tomb and watch over it. I had to protect Tutankhamun.

There was nothing I wanted to do less.

I got up and slipped out of the chamber, tiptoeing quietly through the courtyard. The moon beamed down on me like a torch, guiding me through the village and up on to the mountain. At the top I wished it was less bright. The guards knew about the tomb now and they'd be more watchful than ever. It would not be easy to slip round them tonight.

I inched cautiously forward, creeping from

boulder to boulder till I knew I was safely past them. Then I ran softly down the path to the Valley. In the moonlight I could see the tombs clearly – gaping black holes that followed me like eyes as I edged slowly forwards. Among them, near the centre of the Valley, was Tutankhamun's tomb. In front of it, a thin wisp of smoke curled upwards. The guards had lit a fire and were sitting, cross-legged and watchful, in front of it.

Somehow I had to get to the tomb without them seeing me. But how was I to do that? The Valley was bathed in silver. They'd see me before I even got near.

A hyena howled from the desert. What was I doing in this terrible place? If only I was safe at home with my family. I was about to give up and creep shamefully away when the moon slipped behind a cloud. I had to go on now. Taking a deep breath, I sprinted over to the tomb and crouched down on the opposite side of it from the guards. The moon swung out again. I nearly jumped out of my skin. Four hairy faces were gazing at me. A group of donkeys was tethered just a few feet away.

My mouth went dry. They didn't belong to the guards. So whose were they? Robbers – robbers, of course. Robbers were down there, in the tomb. The guards must have let them in. It was a plot concocted between them. My mind raced. The robbers had ridden here on their donkeys, the guards had unlocked the tomb for them, and now they were down there somewhere, knocking holes in walls, helping themselves to treasure. The guards would have been well paid for their silence. And all I could do was wait till they came out, then try to follow them. If I was lucky, I might discover where they hid the treasure and go for help... if they didn't find me first.

Even now they might be in the burial chamber, their nimble fingers breaking the seals on the great coffin, prising open the lid, pulling aside the linen bandages, reaching in for the priceless jewels and amulets...

What had Grandfather told me? *The King's soul lives so long as his mummy is not harmed.* Had I got here in time? Or was I already too late?

I could hear the guards' voices. One gave a great yawn. "Don't fall asleep," another joked. "It's not morning yet." I clenched my fists. I wanted to jump up and shout out their crime. But I had to keep as still as I could. And wait.

Scared though I was, I hoped it wouldn't be for long. I was struggling to keep my eyes open, and I had to keep them open. I had to stay awake. I fixed them on the steps. I felt my head begin to nod.

A loud rattle woke me from the doze I'd dropped into. My eyes flew open. What was that? Next to me the donkeys stirred uneasily. I peered at the steps. There was something down there, near the grille. I strained my eyes to see. It wasn't the robbers returning. It wasn't a person at all. I licked my dry lips. It was a Thing – a huge winged Thing. It beat its wings helplessly against the wooden bars of the grille. Then it swooped upwards across the pit. It was coming for me!

I flung up my arms to protect my head. My yell would have woken a whole regiment of guards.

"There's someone here!" a voice shouted. Heavy feet pounded towards me. I leapt to my feet to run but I was too late. My arms were seized and pinned behind my back. A torch was shone full in my face. I blinked, screwing up my eyes.

"Why, it's young Ali!" one of the guards

exclaimed. "What are you doing here?"

"Come to rob the tomb I'll be bound," another guard growled. "Where's the rest of your gang?" He gave my arms a yank. Fire shot up them to my shoulders. A gun was pointing at my chest. I fell to my knees in terror.

"Admit it! You're not alone."

They were pretending they didn't know about the robbers! How clever they were!

"I have done nothing wrong. It is them – in there. I dreamt that someone would rob the tomb. That is why I came here. And I am right. They have! They are in the burial chamber. And they have harmed the mummy. I know – I saw his ka, his soul, just now – it flew past me." What was I saying? Why had I mentioned the robbers? These men were part of the gang!

The guards stared at me as if I was mad.

"It was a bat you saw," one of them said. "There are lots of them round here."

"Never mind that!" another said. "What are we going to do with him?"

"Wait till they come out. Shouldn't be long now. They've been in there long enough. They'll know what to do."

I shivered. They were going to hand me over to the robbers. What would happen to me now!

"Here they come!"

Four people were walking slowly up the steps. A torch flashed.

One of the guards ran over to them. I knew that he was telling them about me. A man left the party and hastened over to me. I looked up to see who it was. It was Mr Carter!

I don't know which of us was more startled – him or me. At last he said quietly:

"Why are you here, lad?"

I wanted to ask him the same question. Then I thought. I'd crept secretly into the tomb earlier that day. I was creeping around it again now, at night. He was bound to be as suspicious of me as I was of him.

It is always best to tell the truth. So I told him about my dream. "I came to protect Tutankhamun," I said. "I was afraid the tomb had been robbed." I swallowed and stopped.

Please tell me it hasn't been, my eyes begged him. Please tell me the truth.

Carter's eyes had never left mine. "The King is lucky to have such a devoted servant to watch over him," he said quietly when I'd finished. "But do not worry. There is nothing to fear. I want the world to know about Tutankhamun, and to learn more about your country's glorious past. That is all."

But why was he here now, in the middle

of the night?

"I came to make sure the burial chamber had not been plundered," he explained. "And it hasn't. Tutankhamun is still there, and he is safe." He smiled. "But it was important to keep our visit secret. As soon as it is known that he is here, everyone will want to see him. I cannot allow people to tramp in and out of the tomb. Think of the damage that could be caused to the tomb and its wonderful treasures. We must take great care of it."

"But you will take him away," I said. Grandfather had cried the last time a pharaoh was taken away. I wanted to cry now, too.

Carter leant forward and gripped my hands. "That I will never do. Tutankhamun will remain here, where he belongs. You have my word. Now," he said. "Will you promise me something?"

"If I can," I choked. Ashamed of my tears, I wiped my wet eyes on my sleeve.

"Do not say a word of what you saw this night," he said. "Will you promise me that?"

I nodded.

He smiled. Then he stood up. His hand rested on my head. "It will be a secret between us." I watched him walk rapidly away and say something to the guards. One of them ran over to me.

"Come on, young Ali," he said. He led me over to the fire. "Sit here with us and try to sleep if you can. It will soon be dawn. We will wake you then." Behind me I heard the jangle of harnesses as the four mounted their donkeys. I watched them ride away across the Valley, then I curled up by the fire next to the guards. Already the dark was beginning to lift a little.

A gentle nudge woke me early. "Go home," the guards said. "We don't want to have to explain why you are here. And mind you keep what you have seen to yourself now!" I got up slowly, rubbing my legs, which were stiff from sleeping on the hard ground. I looked down at the tomb. Then I began to run. As I reached the mountain I looked back one more time. "Farewell," I whispered. I didn't know when I'd be back. My stomach was rumbling. I was hungry. If I hurried I might be home in time for breakfast.

HISTORICAL NOTE

On 26 November 1922 Howard Carter, a British archaeologist, pushed a candle through a hole he'd made in an ancient sealed door. An astonishing sight met his eyes. After many years' searching, Carter had finally found his tomb.

It was a find unlike any other. Tutankhamun was a boy when he became pharaoh and only in his teens when he died. Not much is known about his reign. His tomb was a small one by royal standards – probably originally built for someone else. Only the walls of the burial chamber were decorated, and there was evidence that the tomb had been plundered, like other tombs discovered in Egypt's Valley of the Kings. Yet unlike those other tombs, a heap of treasure remained in the four chambers that made up the tomb. And, in the burial chamber, lay the magnificent gold coffin of the boy-king himself, his mummy intact.

A huge task faced Howard Carter. Countless finds needed to be examined, recorded and photographed before they could be transported down the Nile to the Cairo Museum. Carter enlisted experts to help him, but it was months before the first chamber – the 'antechamber' – was cleared and work could begin on the other three.

It must have been difficult. Carter was a careful and thorough archaeologist, but was hampered in his task by the crowds of tourists that now flocked to the Valley. Ever since news had broken of the extraordinary find, the tomb had become a must-see tourist destination. Carter was now famous, but must have wished he wasn't. Everyone wanted to see the tomb's treasures. Tut-mania seized the world. Soon you could buy clothes embroidered with Egyptian designs, or wear imitation Egyptian jewellery, listen to the King Tut record on a gramophone, or even visit an exhibition in London with replicas of the treasures found in the tomb.

Over ninety years later, Tutankhamun continues to fascinate the world, but huge numbers of visitors to his tomb have caused its structure to deteriorate. A replica of it has been built near Howard Carter's house so that visitors may see what the tomb was like without further damage being caused to the original.

Opened in 2014, you can see how the burial chamber would have looked when Carter first looked inside it all those years ago, and gaze on the wonderful golden coffin.

But you won't see Tutankhamun. He still lies in the tomb built for him, thousands of years ago, in the Valley of the Kings.

ACKNOWLEDGEMENTS

A number of people and organizations helped with my research for this book. In particular I'd like to thank: Jaromir Malek, Stephen Quirke, Cat Warsi and – especially – Dr Helen Wickstead for her guidance, encouragement and enthusiasm.